Nice WORK for the CAT and the KING

Nick Sharratt

Chapter 1

Once upon a time there was a king who lived with his best friend, the cat, at 37 Castle Close.

Their previous home had actually been a castle, but I'm sorry to say it was now a ruin, thanks to an Unfortunate Incident involving a bad-tempered, fire-breathing dragon.

The cat and the king were really happy in their new home and they had lovely neighbours:

Mr and Mrs Cromwell

and their two children, Cressida and Christopher.

Anyway, on this particular day the cat and
the king were sitting at the kitchen table. They
had the Royal Money Box in front of them.
The cat was very carefully counting
out their money. The king was
drinking milky tea and
eating toast and honey.

Now perhaps you are thinking that it should
have been the king who was doing the counting.

As a matter of fact he had once had a little
counting house which stood in a corner of
the castle courtyard (before everything was
destroyed in the Unfortunate Incident).

The king was supposed to count his money
in there at the start of every week.

But the king wasn't great at doing sums, so it was the one royal duty he didn't enjoy.

Fortunately the cat loved maths, so he took on the task, and he was the one in charge of the Royal Money Box.

When the cat finished counting he gave the tiniest of sighs.

Sigh!

There hadn't been as many coins to put into piles as he'd hoped for, and they needed coins for lots of things.

They had to pay their bills,

travel on the
Number 23 bus,

do the shopping

and put 50p coins into
the slot of the motorbike
ride at the supermarket.
The king was
very keen on his
motorbike rides.

The cat did some calculations. In less than a fortnight there would be no coins at all left in the Royal Money Box. He didn't say anything (because cats can't talk) but the king caught his eye and knew, as he always did, exactly what his friend was thinking.

"Alack!" cried the king (it was his royal way of saying, "Oh, dear!") Never mind about bills and bus fares: it was awful to think of life without motorbike rides.

But before they could get too depressed, they were distracted by the doorbell.

Chapter 2

It was their neighbours, Mr Cromwell, Cressida and Christopher. They came round to Number 37 every week, so that Cressida could entertain the king with her recorder practice, whilst Christopher played his tambourine. Cressida always made an effort to perform at least one piece chosen especially for the king.

He had his favourite melodies but he also liked anything a bit "royal" so that day she'd decided to play "Good King Wenceslas". Christopher rattled his tambourine and sang along, with Mr Cromwell coming to the rescue when his son forgot the words. The king clapped and cheered with delight (even though it was nowhere near Christmas.)

Then the cat brought out one of his home-made cakes. This one was shaped exactly like the king's crown. It was filled with raspberries and cream, and decorated with jewels made from jelly sweets.

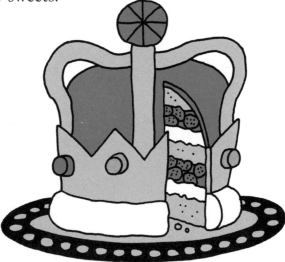

There was a gasp of delight, and then they all tucked in. Everyone agreed that the cake was super-delicious, which would normally have pleased the cat very much.

But today his mind was on other things. If the coins in the Royal Money Box ran out, there'd be no more trips to the supermarket to buy baking ingredients – and that meant no more cake.

That night the cat could hardly sleep a wink. He tossed and turned in his hammock, and tried to work out how they could top up the coins in the Royal Money Box.

The next morning, while the cat and the king were having breakfast, they heard the rattle of the letterbox and the soft thud of something landing on the mat.

The cat darted into the hall and returned with that week's edition of the *Plumchester Times* and a thoughtful look on his face.

He searched through the pages, found what he was looking for and laid the paper down on the table.

"*Job Vacancies*," read the king. "Oh, clever cat! I shall take a job and we will soon have coins aplenty! Now, what would be fit for a king?"

They started reading through the adverts.

BUTCHER

They couldn't see the king working in a
butcher's shop.

BAKER

It would be too hard for the king to resist eating
the cakes and buns. (He had a very sweet tooth.)

CANDLESTICK MAKER

The king hadn't a clue how to make a candlestick.
Neither did the cat (and neither do I,
for that matter.)

LONG-DISTANCE LORRY DRIVER

The king couldn't drive.

WRESTLER

The king didn't fancy that.

ELECTRICIAN

The king didn't even know how to change a light bulb.

At this point, the cat decided to make a list of all the things that the king could actually do. He fetched his laptop, and started to type:

Things at which His Majesty
is especially good:

Waving
Making speeches
Cutting ribbons
Presenting medals
Walking on red carpets
Wearing a heavy crown
Carrying an orb
Carrying a sceptre

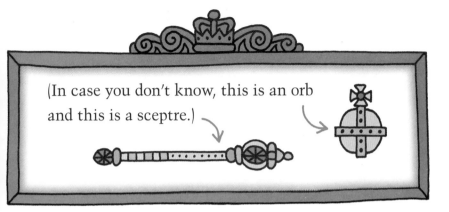

(In case you don't know, this is an orb and this is a sceptre.)

The cat paused.

The king had wandered off and was now resting in his special bejewelled armchair.

The cat typed one more thing:

```
Sitting on a throne.
```

It was rather an odd list, wasn't it? The fact was, the king could do "king things" brilliantly (except for counting). But, up until the Unfortunate Incident, he had always had plenty of servants to take care of everything else.

Now that it was just him and the cat, the king was having to learn how to do a great deal more, but he still needed a lot of practice.

The cat stroked his chin thoughtfully.
He found a felt-tip pen and began circling adverts
in the paper. The first one he ringed was for a

STATION ANNOUNCER

That's the person whose voice you hear
telling you when the trains are arriving and
departing and the stations they'll be stopping at.

The king was particularly good at making
speeches, and the cat reckoned he would be just
as good at making station announcements.

He gently woke the snoozing king and showed
him the advert.

"Bravo!" said the king. "A most
excellent choice! Let us hasten
to the station forthwith!"

Chapter 3

A bus ride later, the cat and the king stood outside Plumchester Railway Station.

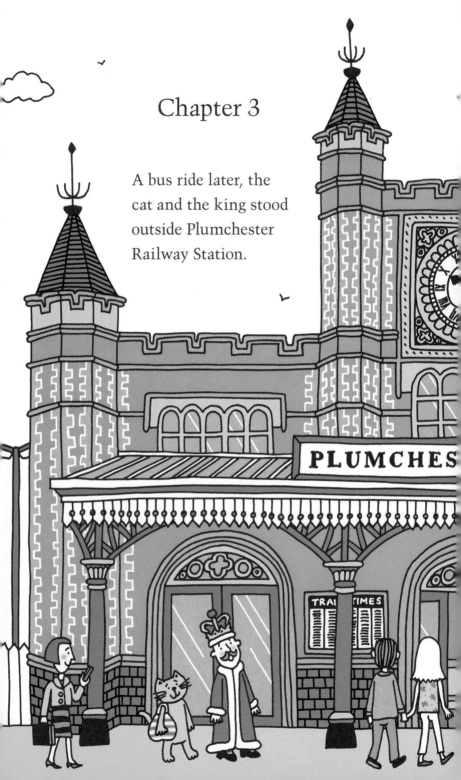

PLUMCHES

TRAIN TIMES

It was a magnificent-looking building, and the king smiled approvingly.

When they found the Station Manager, she
was so excited, she couldn't stop curtseying (the
king often had that effect on people.) She was
even more excited to learn that the king was
interested in the job of Station Announcer.

"In your case, Your Majesty, no interview is
necessary," she gushed. "It would be an honour
if you would care to start work straightaway."

The manager led them up to a little office overlooking the platforms and explained the system to them. There were three computers that flashed up all sorts of information, and a microphone for the king to use for his announcements.

He would need to keep an eye on the computers and inform the passengers about all sorts of things as they cropped up. It was quite a lot to think about, but the king knew he could rely on the cat to help.

They took their seats and the cat studied
the screens. He jotted something down on
one of his sticky notes and passed it across
to the king. It was time for the king's first
announcement! He took a deep breath, leaned
towards the microphone, and said in his most
king-like voice:

We* are royally
delighted to congratulate
the ten thirty-eight
from Pantsby on its
splendidly punctual
arrival.

"Well I never!" said the Station Manager,
looking down on to the platform. "The
passengers are clapping!"

*The king liked to say "We" instead of "I", especially when
speaking in public. It was a "king thing".

The king came to the window and waved graciously to the crowd. (He was particularly skilled at waving.)

The manager was delighted. She'd never had clapping passengers before.

"Excellent work, Your Majesty," she said, and went off to test a new batch of guard's whistles.

It was time for the king's second announcement. The cat passed him a sticky note. He glanced at it, and proclaimed:

It gives us enormous pleasure to declare that the train standing at Platform 2 will be calling at:

Crumblehampton,

Bounceberry,

Flanville East,

Little Widdlington,

Jelly Park

and Flopton-on-Sea.

*Bon voyage** to the ten forty-six and all who ride on her.

*A clever way of saying, "Have a nice trip." It's a bit of French for you.

They listened as the king's amplified words were once again followed by a round of applause and he dashed over to the window to give the crowd another wave. The king and the cat smiled at one another. It was all going very well.

The next hour passed easily,
with announcements and clapping,
and even occasional cheering. The cat
had brought a flask of tea and some slices
of peacock and, in between messages,
they sipped and nibbled.

I should explain that it wasn't real peacock.
It was a cake made by the cat. The body was
carved from coconut sponge and the tail was an
enormous chocolate-chip cookie, cleverly iced to
look like feathers. It had been a lot of work but
the final result was very impressive (and jolly
tasty, too).

But at midday the cat noticed that the signals had failed at Bobblemouth Junction. All the trains were now delayed. He passed a pile of notes to the king, who sighed when he read through them. Making happy announcements was lovely, but giving out bad news was horrid. In his most solemn voice, he declared:

We are royally dismayed to announce that the twelve-fourteen from Gonksham is a miserable fifteen minutes late.

This time, the crowd didn't clap.

The king went on:

We declare with a most heavy heart that the Squigglesford Express is cruelly delayed by twenty long and agonising minutes.

This time the crowd **SOBBED** and **SNIFFLED**.

The king continued:

It is our deeply sorrowful duty to announce the devastating cancellation of the twelve forty-six to Flopton-on-Sea. Our thoughts are with you all at this ghastly, wretched, terrible time.

This time the crowd **WAILED** and **HOWLED**.

At that moment, the Station Manager burst into the room.

STOP, STOP, STOP!

she shouted.

"You're making the passengers cry! Everyone's in floods of tears, and I've had to rush round handing out tissues. Just listen to that din!"

"I'm sorry, Your Majesty, but you're fired."

Chapter 4

They left the station in a hurry, and went and
sat in the town square. The king was looking
rather forlorn, but perked up a little when the cat
produced some egg-and-cress sandwiches he'd
made for their lunch.

When they'd eaten, the cat pulled *The Bumper Book of Jokes* from his bag and, as was their custom after every lunch, the king opened it at random and picked a joke.

"Where do whales get weighed?" he read. "At a whale-weigh station."

He thought for a moment, then grandly proclaimed:

We are NOT amused!

The cat smiled, knowing how much the king loved to say those four words.

He got out his newspaper and showed the king the second job he'd circled. It was a vacancy for a Sales Assistant at Snushell's, Plumchester's smartest department store.

"Bravo!" said the king. "Lead on!"

Snushell's was a very
impressive-looking store.

The king smiled approvingly.

The job vacancy was in the Haberdashery section, which was where you could buy all kinds of items for sewing, like:

needles and pins,

reels of cotton,

buttons and zips

and, best of all . . . lengths of ribbon!

The king, you see, was a bit of an expert at ribbon-cutting.

He'd been required to cut a ribbon every time he'd opened a hospital, or a school, or a library, or a fête:

I declare this hospital open.

I declare this school open.

I declare this library open.

I declare this fête open.

(Kings are always being asked to open things.)

So the cat thought working in Haberdashery might suit the king rather well.

Mr Snushell himself came out to meet them.
He took one look at the king with his fine red
robe, shiny gold crown and sparkling silver
buckles, and gave him the job there and then.

"At Snushell's we pride ourselves on giving
our customers the royal treatment. That should
be no problem for you!" he chortled, as he
headed back to his office.

Snushell's also prided itself on its gorgeous displays. The centrepiece of the Haberdashery department was a rather spectacular maypole, designed to show off the store's range of ribbons and trimmings. The cat and the king admired it as they crossed over to their counter.

The cat checked out the till. He was looking forward to counting out the customers' change. The king, meanwhile, had found the drawer where the tape measure and scissors were kept. In the twinkling of an eye he picked up the scissors and headed straight for the display.

"We hereby take great delight in the cutting of these ribbons," he declared triumphantly and, with an expert swish of the scissors, he went:

snip,

snip,

snip,

snip,

snip,

snip!

Before the cat could stop him, he'd cut through each and every ribbon.

Things got into a bit of a tangle.

Mr Snushell came running. "Look at my maypole!" he cried. "And look at my customers!

"You were meant to treat them like royalty, and instead we have muddle and mayhem. King or no king, you're fired!"

The cat and the king slunk away, and Mr
Snushell began the fiddly task of untying everyone.

Chapter 5

The cat and the king were relieved to get back home. It was a shame that today hadn't gone quite as well as planned, but the cat had already circled another couple of possible jobs in the paper, including one for an Attendant at Plumchester Museum. Part of the job involved giving stickers to visitors to show they'd paid their entrance fee. The king was very good at presenting medals, and the cat thought that giving people stickers would be quite similar.

Whilst the king had a nap on his throne, the cat set about baking a brand new cake. It was a fruit cake, shaped and iced to look like an Egyptian mummy case. That seemed appropriate, because he'd seen there was a special exhibition at the museum all about ancient Egypt!

Early next morning, they caught
the bus into town and got
off at the museum.

TREASURES
— OF —
ANCIENT
EGYPT

TREASURES
— OF —
ANCIENT
EGYPT

MUS

It was a splendid-looking building,
and the king smiled
approvingly.

A lady dressed all in black greeted them.
She gave them the key to the till and a roll of
stickers, and ran through a long list of important
rules and regulations. I'm sorry to say that
the king wasn't really concentrating. He was
distracted by the glittering Egyptian treasures
that could be glimpsed through the doorway to
one side of the entrance hall. He could see lots of
gold, and gold was his absolute favourite colour.

At ten o'clock the museum opened its doors and the first visitors came pouring in. They were a school party, come to see the special exhibition.

The cat and the king recognised the red-and-grey uniforms and, sure enough, they soon spotted Christopher Cromwell, the little boy who lived next door in Castle Close.

They gave him a quick wave and
Christopher waved back, but then
it was time to start work. The king
picked up the stickers, and the cat
made for the till.

The teacher in charge paid for everyone by
handing over two carrier bags full of coins. It
was just as well the cat liked counting!

By the time he had finished, the entrance
hall was empty. The whole school had gone into
the exhibition – and the king was nowhere to
be seen. The cat was puzzled. He pondered for
a moment, then went to peep through the
doorway. An extraordinary sight met his eyes.

The king was perched on a magnificent
gold throne. In front of him stood a long and
very well-behaved queue of children, teachers
and helpers. The room was strangely quiet.
The little girl at the head of the queue stepped
forward and burtsied.

(For those of you who don't already know, a burtsey is a cross between a bow and a curtsey. It was invented by Christopher Cromwell and he often gave his classmates burtseying lessons in the playground at lunchtime.)

The king nodded graciously and gently pressed a sticker on to the girl's jumper.

She burtsied again and stepped aside. Then the next child came up and the ritual was repeated.

When it was the turn of the adults they dropped to their knees to make it easier for the king to give them their stickers.

It was all very solemn and dignified, until . . .

NOOOOOOOO!!!

The lady in black
came rushing
into the room.

"WHAT ON EARTH DO
YOU THINK YOU ARE DOING?
King Ickytumtum's throne is four thousand
years old and absolutely priceless. It is
completely and utterly against the rules to sit
on it. HOW DARE YOU!"

"You're fired!" she snapped,
and she marched the
king right out of
the museum.

The king was a bit upset.
He really couldn't see what
he'd done that was so wrong:
after all, he had a throne of
his own back at Number 37
(even if it was home-made).

And there'd been a
genuine gold throne in
his castle, in the days
before the Unfortunate
Incident. He was an
expert in throne-sitting.

The cat and the king waited for the bus home. When it arrived, the cat thought a little royal waving from the back seat might help matters.

He was right. The king soon cheered up considerably. The cat, meanwhile, thought about the one remaining job that he'd circled in the paper. What would they do if that didn't work out?

Chapter 6

Next morning, round at 35 Castle Close, the Cromwells were discussing their royal neighbours over breakfast.

Mr Cromwell's cousin Keith worked in the ticket office at the railway station and had witnessed the commotion there the day before.

Mrs Cromwell's best friend Bev had got tangled up in the ribbons at Snushell's.

Christopher had actually been there with the rest of his class when the king was ordered to leave the museum.

"The poor king! It can't be easy for him to find work," said Mrs Cromwell.

"I suppose blue blood's not much help when it comes to normal jobs," shrugged her husband, reaching for the peanut butter. "Neither's being born with a silver spoon in your mouth," he mumbled, his own mouth being rather full of toast.

Mr Cromwell liked the king, but he did think he was rather posh.

Christopher was just about to ask his dad what on earth he was talking about when Cressida spotted the cat and the king walking by.

"They're out early," said Mrs Cromwell as they all waved from the window. "Must be heading off for another job interview."

And, indeed, they were.

The final job that the cat had spotted was for a Doorman at The Grand, Plumchester's most luxurious hotel, which they passed each time they took the bus into town. The cat had noticed that the steps leading up to the front entrance were covered in red carpet.

Walking on red carpets is something that kings are specially trained to do.

The cat thought the king would feel very much at home working in such a place.

They got off the bus
outside the hotel.

The king smiled approvingly as they walked up the red-carpeted steps.

He smiled approvingly as they
entered the red-and-gold lobby.

The manager smiled approvingly when he saw the king, thinking he colour co-ordinated beautifully with The Grand.

"We normally expect our doorman to wear a uniform," he said, "but you will add even more class dressed just as you are. Is that crown real gold?"

"Most assuredly," replied the king.

The manager explained all about being a doorman, and the king thought it sounded right up his street.

- He would be required to stand at the top of the carpeted steps looking splendid: that was easy enough.

- He would need to order taxis to stop. Well, giving orders came quite naturally to kings.

- And he would have to open the door for arriving and departing guests.

It was true that, before the Unfortunate Incident, the king had always had a servant to open any door; but since then he had become rather good at opening them himself. He even quite enjoyed it.

The manager then turned to the cat. If it were of interest, he said, the hotel was also looking for an extra bellboy – or bellcat – to carry luggage to and from guests' rooms. The cat was delighted. He thought it would be an excellent way for him to keep an eye on the king.

The king went to take up his position by the entrance and the cat popped on his bellboy hat. The receptionist immediately sent him off to collect the suitcases of the guests who had been staying in the hotel's most luxurious suite and who were now checking out.

The couple from the penthouse were very glamorous looking. The lady wore lots of sparkly jewellery and so did her husband.

The cat returned with their baggage and followed them out of the hotel.

He saw how gracious the king was when he held the door open for the lady and gentleman.

He saw how impressive the king was when he raised his arm, snapped his fingers and straightaway stopped a taxi.

He saw how charming the king was when he helped them into the cab, gently closed the passenger door and, as the taxi sped away, waved them goodbye.

But the cat had spotted another thing, too: the unhappy looks on the faces of the lady and gentleman. It had actually seemed as if they were rather cross with the king. Turn back the page and check again for yourself.

Before the cat had a chance to think about this, another taxi pulled up. The king was there in a flash to welcome another stylish lady and gentleman to the hotel.

The cat felt the king made an excellent doorman, but again he saw frowns on the new arrivals' faces.

The same thing happened with all the guests who checked in or out of the hotel over the next couple of hours. The king was as gracious and charming as he could be, but all he got in return were . . .

grumpy looks,

sullen stares

and furious expressions.

The hotel manager had also noticed the rather disagreeable atmosphere in the lobby. He called the king and the cat into his office.

"The problem is this," he said to the king. "The guests are upset that you are outshining them with your regal robe and, in particular, with your magnificent gold crown. *They* like to be the ones with the best clothes and the finest jewels. I must insist that you wear the doorman's uniform and cap instead."

"We are sorry," replied the king, "but the royal crown does not come off."

It was a fact: the king had been wearing the crown for as long as he could remember, and it was now so firmly wedged on his head that it was impossible to remove it – even at bathtime and bedtime.

"In that case," the manager said, "I regret to say you're both fired."

Chapter 7

The cat and the king returned home feeling
rather gloomy. They had some spaghetti
with pesto sauce for lunch and, even
though it was their favourite
meal, it didn't really help.

The king reached for
*The Bumper Book of
Jokes*, opened it and
read, "What did
the witch do at
the hotel? She
ordered broom
service."

He shut the book, said wearily, "We are not
amused," and went and slumped on his throne.

The cat had to agree about the joke. He stayed in the kitchen and spent the afternoon making a unicorn out of poppyseed cake, decorated with lemon frosting.

He usually found baking very relaxing, but today he couldn't stop fretting: none of the king's jobs had worked out and the number of coins in the Royal Money Box was getting lower and lower.

When the king came in
for tea the unicorn cake
brought a big smile to his face.
It did look amazing and the
cat was pretty pleased with it,
too, although the horn wasn't
quite right. (It should really
have been an ice-cream
cornet but he'd had to make do with a banana.)

They were just about to tuck in when the
doorbell rang.

It was Mrs Cromwell with Cressida and Christopher. Mrs Cromwell said she had some news that she thought might be of interest. The king gestured for them to sit down and the cat made drinks and cut them some unicorn.

Mrs Cromwell put down her tea, took a deep breath, and said, "Your Majesty, an important job vacancy has just come up. It's for a lollipop man or lady to work outside the children's school.

"It's a highly responsible job, making sure everybody crosses the road safely, and requires a very special person to do it. Cressida and Christopher wondered whether Your Majesty might be that special person?"

The two children nodded enthusiastically between mouthfuls of cake.

The king smiled, but said nothing. Mrs Cromwell pressed on. "It would be for a couple of hours a day, Monday to Friday, at the start and finish of school. Your Majesty would be provided with a high-visibility jacket – and a lollipop sign, of course."

The king wasn't sure. Having been fired four times already that week, he'd lost some of his confidence. He looked over to the cat for advice.

The cat pondered.

- •The king did rather like being the centre of attention and the very bright jacket would be excellent for that.

- • He was practised at giving commands, so stopping traffic and instructing children when to cross should be easy-peasy.

- • He was highly skilled at sceptre-holding.

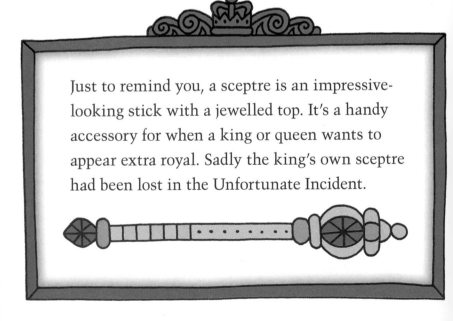

Just to remind you, a sceptre is an impressive-looking stick with a jewelled top. It's a handy accessory for when a king or queen wants to appear extra royal. Sadly the king's own sceptre had been lost in the Unfortunate Incident.

It seemed to the cat that holding a lollipop sign might be just as much fun for the king as holding a sceptre, maybe even more fun, since a lollipop sign was bigger and more eye-catching.

So he gave the king a thumbs-up or, to be strictly accurate, a toes-up, since cats don't have thumbs, or even fingers.

The king said he would be most interested in the job. Mrs Cromwell looked very pleased and the children bounced up and down with excitement.

Mrs Cromwell then turned to the cat: she had some news for him, too. Her good friend Monsieur Dupont was about to open a little café in the high street.

Because Monsieur Dupont was from France, the place would be decorated with French posters,

the sandwiches would be made with French bread

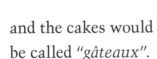

and the cakes would be called "*gâteaux*".

What Monsieur Dupont needed for the grand
opening at the weekend, however, was an extra-
special cake or *"gâteau"* to go on display and
attract lots of attention. Perhaps, suggested
Mrs Cromwell, the cat could make him one?
Monsieur Dupont would pay him, of course.

The cat did not have to think twice. He gave
an eager toes-up sign.

Mrs Cromwell beamed, the children clapped
and the king cried, "Bravo!"

When the cat showed their guests to the
door he was already pondering on ideas for the
perfect cake for Monsieur Dupont.

Chapter 8

It was the king's first morning as a lollipop man.
He wore a fluorescent yellow jacket over his robe
and in his hand he gripped a STOP sign that
really did look like an enormous lollipop.

At eight-fifteen sharp, the cat and the king walked round to the zebra crossing on School Lane, and there they stood waiting for the first children to arrive.

The king was not keen on waiting and would have happily got on with ordering the traffic to stop anyway, but the cat made him stay put on the pavement until he actually had someone to guide across the road.

At last they heard sounds of chatter and laughter and everyone seemed to arrive at once, including Cressida and Christopher with their dad.

It was time for the king to take command. The crowd fell silent as they watched him scan the road for a break in the traffic.

He looked right . . . and left . . . and right again.

Then he stepped off the kerb and strode forward, head held high and lollipop thrust out in front of him.

Standing proudly in the middle of the crossing, he gestured with his free hand for everyone to cross.

Cressida, Christopher and Mr Cromwell led the way, marching in perfect time with one another.

As they approached the king they saluted, even Mr Cromwell, who would never normally do such a thing (and he most definitely did not go in for bowing, curtseying or burtseying.)

Today, however, he just couldn't help himself. The king saluted smartly back.

Everyone else fell into line
behind the Cromwells, joining
in the march and saluting the
king. The waiting drivers tootled
their horns in encouragement.

TOOT!

TOOT!

When the parade was over and everyone was safely on the school side, the king returned to the opposite kerb and the cars that had come to a halt started moving again.

Already more people had arrived and were waiting excitedly for the king to help them cross. The king had a big smile on his face: he was clearly enjoying himself and the cat was delighted.

By nine o'clock all the children had made it to school and the pavements were empty again. It was time for the king and the cat to leave, although the king was a little reluctant. He was already looking forward to returning at going-home time.

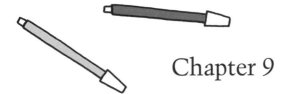

Chapter 9

Back at Number 37 it was time to start work on Monsieur Dupont's cake. The cat had thought long and hard, and had decided to create something unforgettably spectacular: an edible Eiffel Tower, made from three creamy *gâteaux* and a lot of crunchy gingerbread. He'd drawn himself a diagram of it.

strawberry gâteau

iced gingerbread

cherry gâteau

chocolate gâteau

The cat was pleased with his sketch, but turning it into a reality wasn't exactly going to be a piece of cake (if you'll pardon the joke).

Thankfully the king was there to help.
Starting with the *gâteaux*, between them they

weighed

and sifted

and stirred

and licked out
the bowl,

and rinsed

and stoned

and melted

and licked out
the bowl,

and whisked

and greased

and poured

and licked out
the bowl.

With the three sponges baking in the oven, it was time to make the gingerbread. There wasn't a bowl big enough for all the dough they needed, so they mixed it up in their wheelbarrow (having given it a good clean first.)

The cat rolled out some of the dough on the kitchen table and cut out the first of the four sides of the tower.

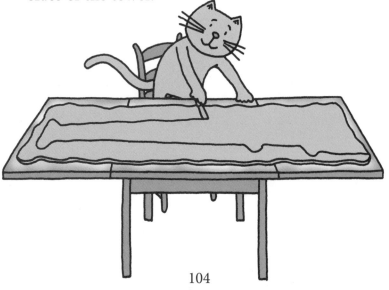

It was only then that he realised
something rather important:
there was absolutely no way
the gingerbread shapes
were going to fit into
the oven!

The pair of them were scratching their chins
over this matter when all at once it went very
dark in the kitchen, as if night had suddenly
fallen. Wondering what was blocking out the
light, the cat and the king turned towards the
window, and saw . . .

Chapter 10

They rushed to bolt the back door but
it was too late: the dragon was
already squeezing its way
into the kitchen.

It glowered at the cat and the king, breathing heavily, smoke trickling from its nostrils. It didn't look the least bit friendly.

A sound like thunder filled the room:

RRRRRRRRRRRUMBLE!!

It was coming from the dragon's tummy. It meant that the dragon was hungry.

The cat and the king were horror-stricken. They knew this creature only too well.

RAARGH!

It was the very same dragon who had burnt down their castle in the Unfortunate Incident.

And, as if that wasn't enough, it had also paid a visit to Number 37 once before, and had very nearly set the place alight.

It was only thanks to Mr and Mrs Cromwell that there hadn't been a second Unfortunate Incident. (They'd sprayed the dragon with cola to put out its flames.)

After that close shave the cat had done plenty of research into bright-red, green-eyed, fire-breathing dragons.

He knew (and perhaps you know this, too) that they were greedy creatures, and at their most dangerous when they felt hungry.

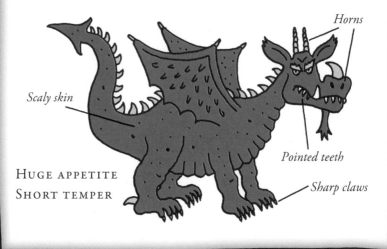

Horns

Scaly skin

Pointed teeth

HUGE APPETITE
SHORT TEMPER

Sharp claws

He knew that they were fussy eaters. They
hated sweet things and really only liked
food that tasted smoky.

P R E F E R R E D   D I E T :

Smoked meat

Smoked fish

Smoked cheese

Smoky-bacon-
flavoured crisps

As the king stood there trembling, the cat
cast his eyes around the kitchen, searching in
desperation for some food to offer the dragon.
Gingerbread dough or half-cooked sponge
wouldn't do; it had to be smoky-tasting.

He couldn't think of anything suitable in the cupboard or in the fridge. And there wasn't even any cola left for emergency fire-fighting. It seemed like a hopeless situation.

The dragon was horribly close now. Flickers of flame escaped from between its fangs.

 Just then the cat glanced at
the spice rack on the wall. He
and the king had bought it at
a car boot sale some time
ago and it was lined with
little jars containing all sorts of herbs and spices.

With his sharp eyesight, the cat homed in on
the labels:

(They'd just been using
ginger in their baking.)

SMOKED Paprika!

The cat leapt across the room and grabbed the jar.

Wrenching off the lid, he threw the entire contents into the dragon's open mouth.

Whooooosh!

Now, if that had happened to you or me, I don't think we'd have been very happy. Paprika is such a hot spice it needs to be used in very small quantities, not whole jarfuls. The dragon was taken completely by surprise. It coughed and sneezed when the dark-red powder flew down its throat, and the cat wondered nervously if he'd done the right thing.

But the dragon soon recovered. It licked its lips with its long black tongue and, slowly but surely, a huge contented smile spread across its face. It even started purring. (If you've never heard a dragon purr, imagine the loud BRRRM-BRRRM sound of a sports car.) It had clearly enjoyed its unexpected snack very much indeed.

The cat sighed with relief and the king stopped shaking. The crisis was over.

Phew!

The dragon made itself comfortable on the kitchen floor. It seemed in no hurry to leave and, as it was now in such a good mood, the cat and the king felt able to get on with their work.

The sponges had baked nicely, but they still had to work out how to cook the gingerbread.

They looked at the enormous shape on the table,

and they looked at the far-too-small oven. What a conundrum!

The dragon had been watching them with interest. Now it rose up, padded over to the table and inspected the rolled-out dough for itself.

With one neatly aimed burst of flame, it cooked the gingerbread to perfection in a matter of seconds.

BWOOOM!

The cat clapped his paws and the king cheered, "Huzzah!" and, "Bravo!" and, "Jolly good show!" The dragon was rather pleased with itself.

It stayed long enough to bake the other
pieces of the tower for them, then made its way
back into the garden. (It was off to a beach
barbecue at Flopton-on-Sea.) Just before
it took off, the cat whispered
something in its ear.

What it actually said was,
"Miaow, miaow, miaow,"
but the dragon understood
exactly and nodded its
head enthusiastically.

The cat and the king waved as their new friend soared towards the clouds, then they hurried back inside. They had to get the tower finished because the grand opening was the very next day – and of course the king had his lollipop-man job to do as well.

Chapter 11

It was the day of the grand opening. Monsieur Dupont stood outside his café with the Cromwell family, who all looked very smart, dressed in their best clothes, and sporting medals that the king had given them. They'd come to lend a hand, but right now they were twiddling their thumbs and wondering about the same two things:

1) where was the cat and his special cake?
2) would any customers actually turn up?

Monsieur Dupont looked
nervously at his watch.

Suddenly Christopher noticed something high in the sky. Was it a bird? Was it a plane?

No, it was a bright-red dragon, with an Eiffel Tower gripped in its claws and two passengers balanced precariously on its back!

*"Oh là là!"** exclaimed an excited
Monsieur Dupont. The Cromwells didn't
know what to say – last time they'd met
that dragon it had been a real troublemaker.
They watched open-mouthed as it came closer.

All at once people started arriving from every
direction. They'd all seen the same extraordinary
sight and were running to investigate.

*His way of saying, "Wow!" A bit more French for you.

The dragon came in to land. It hovered in front of the café and very gently set the Eiffel Tower on a table top.

The king carefully jumped down and the cat followed him.

Once they were firmly back on the ground, the cat handed the king a shiny gold medal on a ribbon, which the king duly placed around the dragon's neck as a thank you for all its help.

The delighted dragon took off into the sky and was gone – but not before treating the crowd to a quick burst of fancy flame-throwing.

The crowd was really big now, with quite a few familiar faces. They all turned their attention to the magnificent Eiffel Tower, which was giving off the most delicious gingerbready smell and making everybody extremely hungry. A delighted Monsieur Dupont decided it was time to open for business.

He asked the king to step forward and handed him a pair of scissors, as Cressida and Christopher unfurled the ribbon they'd brought with them.

The king proclaimed:

It is with the utmost pleasure that we declare this café well and truly open!

He snipped the ribbon and the crowd cheered:

HOORAY!

Chapter 12

It was the most successful day. There were lots and lots of customers and Monsieur Dupont couldn't have been happier. When it was all over, he said, *"Merci beaucoup,"** to the king and to the Cromwells,

and he warmly congratulated the cat on the edible Eiffel Tower which had been such a hit.

* That's how you say, "Thank you very much," in French.
There you go – you can practically speak the language now!

Everyone who had come had been given
a little piece, and now all that was left was
a handful of crumbs. Monsieur Dupont was
extremely keen for the cat to make lots more
spectacular cakes for the café in the future.
The cat thought that sounded marvellous.

So it all turned out splendidly in the end. The
king had found a job he really enjoyed and the cat
had found one, too. Between them
they would be able to make sure
that the Royal Money Box
always had enough coins
in it. Huzzah!

On the way home the cat and the king popped
into the supermarket and the king had three
goes on the motorbike ride to celebrate.

And whilst the king was enjoying his rides, the cat went and bought lots of little jars of smoked paprika . . .

. . . just in case.

Gingerbread Cats

Always ask an adult to help you
when you're cooking.

✳ ✳ ✳   Ingredients: ✳ ✳ ✳

350g plain flour

2 tsp ground ginger

1 tsp bicarbonate of soda

100g butter, cut into little pieces

175g soft light-brown sugar

1 egg, beaten

4 tbsp golden syrup

Raisins or currants

Writing icing

✳ ✳ ✳   Here's what you do: ✳ ✳ ✳

• Pre-heat the oven to 190°C/375°F/Gas 5

• In a big bowl, stir
the flour, ginger
and bicarbonate
of soda together.

- Use your fingers to rub the butter into the flour mixture, until it looks like fine breadcrumbs.

- Stir in the brown sugar, then add the syrup and egg. Mix it with a fork, then with your hands, till it makes a firm dough.

- Roll the dough out to about 5mm thick. To stop it sticking, roll it between two layers of cling film.

- Cut out circles using a smooth cookie cutter, or a glass or tumbler.

- To make cat shapes, cut a section like this out of each circle.

- Line a baking tray with baking parchment, then carefully space your biscuits out on it. You may need a second baking tray.

- Press currant eyes and a nose on to each biscuit.

- Pop the biscuits in the fridge for 20 minutes before you bake them.

- Bake for 10-12 minutes until the biscuits are golden brown and still a bit soft to the touch.

- Let the biscuits cool on the tray for a couple of minutes, then transfer them to a wire rack to cool completely.

- Use the writing icing to give each cat a mouth and whiskers.

Your biscuits are now ready to eat. Huzzah!

For Lindsey

First published in the UK in 2018 by Alison Green Books
An imprint of Scholastic Children's Books
Euston House, 24 Eversholt Street, London NW1 1DB
A division of Scholastic Ltd
www.scholastic.co.uk
London – New York – Toronto – Sydney – Auckland
Mexico City – New Delhi – Hong Kong

ISBN: 978 1 407178 88 2

1 3 5 7 9 8 6 4 2

The moral rights of Nick Sharratt have been asserted.

Papers used by Scholastic Children's Books are made from
wood grown in sustainable forests.